The Adventures of

# Titch & Mitch

# The Adventures of
# Titch & Mitch

## Book 5
## The Blue Wizard

## Garth Edwards
### Illustrated by Max Stasyuk

INSIDE
POCKET

Published in Great Britain by Inside Pocket Publishing Limited

First published in Great Britain in 2010

A CIP catalogue record for this book is available from the British Library

ISBN 978-0-9562315-4-3

Inside Pocket Publishing Limited Reg. No. 06580097

Printed and bound in Great Britain by CPI Bookmarque Ltd, Croydon

www.insidepocket.co.uk

For N & J

# Contents

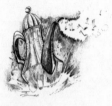

Castle of Father Christmas

Hospital Tree

Plum Tree

Cottage T.H.

Beaver's Dam

Apple Tree

Rock Pool

Lake

Beach

Waterfall

King's Castle

Island Map

# 1

# The Singing Kettle

IT WAS A LOVELY SUMMER'S DAY WHEN TITCH
and Mitch landed their magic bicycle on the roof of
Wendy's house. The pixies liked to visit their special
friend about mid-morning, because it was then the
little girl had tea and cakes in her playroom. She lived
in the village next to the wood where Wiffen the
intelligent turkey had his cottage.

"Are you ready Titch?" called out Mitch.

Apart from the strawberry tarts made by Wendy's
mother, the best thing about visiting Wendy's house
was the slide down the chimney.

"Coming," replied Titch, as he tied the bicycle
safely to the television aerial on the roof. Sitting side

by side on top of the
chimney pot, the two
brothers shouted out,
"Ready, steady,
GO!" Then
they
launched
themselves
down into
the
darkness
below.

Usually, Wendy
left her doll's house facing
the fireplace so the pixies could slide out of the
chimney and into the front door of the little house.
But on this occasion, Wendy's mother, doing a spot
of cleaning, had moved the doll's house and in its
place left a mop and a bucket of dirty water. The
pixies whooshed down the chimney, slid out onto the
carpet, tripped over the mop and fell straight into the
waiting bucket.

"Yarroo!" squealed Titch in alarm, as he landed
with a sploosh! in the cold, dirty water.

"Yikes," spluttered Mitch, crashing on top of his
brother. They both flapped and splashed around in

the bucket until Wendy came running into the room.

"Be quiet!" she cried. "Mummy will hear you and get the broom out again." Once before, Wendy's mother had caught sight of the pixies and, being a little short-sighted, had thought they were rats and so chased them all round the room with a broom.

The little girl rescued the pixies from the bucket and dried them off with a soft white towel.

"I'm very sorry," she said, "but I've had my tea and strawberry cakes already, and now I'm going to Mandy Jones' birthday party. It's a fancy dress party, with a barbeque being held in the woods. Daddy is taking me there now."

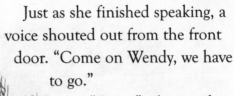

Just as she finished speaking, a voice shouted out from the front door. "Come on Wendy, we have to go."

"Oops," whispered Wendy. "Sorry! Can't stop." In a flash she had gone, leaving two damp and bedraggled pixies sitting on the floor, looking forlorn and feeling very sorry for themselves.

"I know, we'll go and see Wiffen!" said Mitch. "He's always doing something interesting."

"I hope there's a squirrel in the garden," Titch sniffed anxiously. The best way of getting back to their magic bicycle on the roof was to persuade a passing

squirrel to let them ride on its
back as it shimmied up the
drainpipe.

"We'll have to find
something to give it though,"
added Mitch.

It took Titch just a few
minutes to explore the house
and find a big, juicy plum in a
fruit bowl.

Mitch went to the open
widow and leaned out. "Squirrel, oh squirrel," he
shouted. "Where are you?"

Barely a second later, a large red squirrel with
bright eyes scampered down from a nearby tree and
said, "Hello pixies, what do you want?"

"We need a ride to the roof top," called back
Mitch.

The squirrel's eyes narrowed. "Have you got anything good to eat?" he asked, rather shrewdly.

Titch held out the plum. "This is for you, when we both get back to our bicycle."

The squirrel was delighted. He zoomed up the drainpipe carrying the pixies back to the roof of the house, then scampered away happily with his reward.

Later that morning, Titch and Mitch landed their magic bicycle at the little stone cottage that Wiffen shared with Perry, the Old English sheepdog.

They stopped by a tree and waited. Wiffen was standing in the doorway talking to a rather scruffy looking gnome, who was pushing a little cart full of pots and pans.

Seeing them, Wiffen waved a wing and called out joyfully, "Hello chaps! I won't be long. This tinker gnome wants to sell me a kettle."

"But it's a special kettle," insisted the gnome. "It's a singing kettle, and worth a lot of money."

"Nonsense," replied Wiffen. "All I want is hot water to make a pot of tea. There's nothing special about that! And anyway, kettles do not sing. Sometimes they can whistle, but they certainly never sing. I shall give you one penny for it, and if you don't like it you can be on your way."

"It's worth a lot more...." protested the gnome.

"Perry," ordered Wiffen, turning to his shaggy friend. "Growl at this smelly creature."

Lifting one ear and half opening a sleepy eye, Perry tried to growl. But his heart wasn't in it and it sounded more like a polite cough.

Wiffen glared at him, but Perry had already gone back to sleep.

"All right, all right," conceded the gnome. "You can have it for a penny."

After the gnome had gone, Wiffen invited the two pixie brothers inside for a drink. "You can be the first to have tea from my new kettle," he said triumphantly, lighting the stove.

When the kettle started to boil, there came a familiar whistling sound, but before Wiffen could turn off the heat, the kettle started to sing in a high trilling voice.

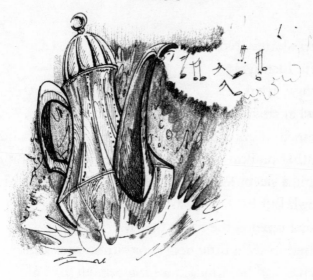

*"There's a hedgehog in your garden,*
*With a little pot in hand.*
*Expect a knock on your front door,*
*And there you'll see him stand!"*

When it had finished, the shrill voice reverted to its whistling. Wiffen turned off the gas quickly and stared at the kettle.

"Well I never!" he said at last. "The kettle was singing... something about a hedgehog."

"He said a hedgehog is about to knock on your door," laughed Mitch.

"And if he does," added Titch, "then the kettle can tell the future. Wouldn't that be something!"

"Rubbish!" responded Wiffen, flapping his

feathers about. "Nobody can tell the future. Least of
all an old kettle!"

At that moment, there came a very loud knock. They
all jumped up in surprise and stared at the front door.

Gathering himself, Wiffen snorted loudly. "Don't
worry," he reassured them. "Whoever it is, it won't be
a hedgehog."

As he opened the door, they were all quite
surprised to see a little hedgehog sitting back on his
haunches and holding out a little pot. He had a
pleading look on his face and said, in a soft voice,
"Please Mr Wiffen, can you let me have a little bit of

sugar. I seem to have run out."
Instead of telling the
hedgehog to go and
pester somebody else, as
he would normally have
done, Wiffen quietly took
the pot from the hedgehog's
paws and silently walked to
his kitchen. He filled the pot
with some sugar and, returning to
the front door, gave it back without a word.

"Thank you ever so much!" said the little fellow,
and scampered away into the long grass.

When Wiffen had closed the door, the three
stared at each other in amazement.

"So I was right. The kettle can tell the future," said
Titch.

"It's a valuable kettle after
all," added Mitch.

"Nonsense!"
screeched Wiffen,
recovering his
composure. "It's just
a coincidence. Kettles
can't tell the future."

"Let's have some

tea now then," said Titch quietly. "Will you put the kettle back on?"

"Of course," said Wiffen. "But it won't happen a second time."

The three of them watched as the kettle started to boil again. It began to whistle gently, then it got louder and the whistling changed to the shrill voice once more.

*"Stay indoors, don't go out,*
*There's thunder and there's rain about!"*

Increasingly impatient, Wiffen snapped off the gas and the kettle gurgled into silence.

"What poppycock!" he exclaimed. "Balderdash! It's not going to rain." He went to the window and threw it open. "See? There's blue sky everywhere," he chortled. "It's nonsense. Utter nonsense! I'll prove it to you. I'll go outside to show you it's nonsense."

He stomped out of the cottage with his feathers all ruffled. Titch and Mitch watched him through the window. In the garden, the turkey strutted about, flapping his wings and looking at the sky.

"No chance of rain," he called out. Then he did a little turkey dance by tucking his red wattle down by his neck and spreading his tail feathers out wide. He hopped from one foot to the other several times then bent his head right down to the ground and waggled

his tail feathers from side to side. Finally, he did a
little jump into the air and spun round to finish his
dance. Now he was facing the cottage and looking up
into the sky on the far side.

As the pixies watched, a look of horror came over
the bird's face. "Oh-oh," he said,
and pointed his wing
feathers upwards. The
sky was split by a
sudden flash of
lightning, followed
sharply by a great
rumble of thunder.
Huge black clouds
tumbled over the

cottage and a heavy rain started to fall. In an instant, Wiffen was drenched to the bone. With a desperate squawk, he raced back to the cottage and tumbled in through the front door.

Defeated, he collapsed on the floor in a sodden heap, leaving a trail of rainwater behind him.

The pixies laughed at the sorry looking creature before them.

"Now do you believe the kettle can tell the future?" asked Titch, chortling with glee.

Through beady eyes, Wiffen glared at them both.

The storm was short lived and soon the sun came out again. By this time, Wiffen had dried himself off and cheered up. They all agreed that the kettle could tell the future, and Wiffen was now delighted with his purchase and was busy making plans for what was yet to be. He was eager to know if the kettle could answer questions about what was going to happen, or did it just pop up with weather forecasts and simple little bits of information.

"I'm not sure I want to know what's going to happen in the future," said Mitch nervously.

"Yes, some things are best left well alone," agreed Titch. "Although there are a few things I'd like to know about."

"Well, I want to know everything that's going to happen, and I'll make that kettle boil water all day if necessary!" said Wiffen.

"Let's boil it again right now, and I'll ask it a pertinent question," he announced, striking a match to light the gas.

As the water heated up, they all stood around it, watching and waiting.

After a short while, the water started to boil and the kettle started to whistle. Wiffen opened his beak to ask a question but, before he could say a word, the kettle started to sing.

*"I see a person coming this way,*
*In a long black cloak and a pointed hat.*
*She's looking for two pixies, a turkey and a dog,*
*But I can't tell you any more than that!"*

With that, the kettle stopped singing and resumed whistling.

Wiffen was puzzled. "Who do we know who wears a long black cloak and wears a pointed hat?" he asked, thoughtfully.

Titch just sat frozen with a look of horror on his face.

Mitch tried to speak, but although his mouth opened and closed, no noise came out except for the chattering of his teeth and his face went very pale.

Wiffen frowned at them. "What's the matter with you two? Can't you speak? I said, 'Who do

we know who wears a long black coat and a pointed hat?'"

He was about to say 'Has the cat got your tongue?' but he didn't. Realisation had dawned on him. His beak started to tremble and his little black eyes opened very wide indeed. "The Black Witch," he squeaked hoarsely.

Then he roared in fright. "THE BLACK WITCH IS COMING HERE!"

Fluffing up his feathers frantically, he began to stumble about the little room. "RUN," he gobbled. "FLEE! HIDE! Run for your LIVES!"

They didn't know what to do until Titch shouted, "To the woods, we can hide in the woods."

Mitch ran to the window and looked out. "It's too late," he cried. "I can see her. She's coming out of the woods."

It was all too much for Wiffen. One of the things that really frightened him was the Black Witch, so he dived under the table to hide. Unfortunately, although his head and wings fitted under the table his bottom feathers stuck out into the room. Woken by the commotion, Perry dived under the table as well, causing a great deal of wriggling and shuffling from Wiffen. "There's no room for you Perry," he gobbled. "Go away."

But the dog stayed under the table and squeezed Wiffen's bottom even further out into the room.

"Get your magic feather ready Mitch," warned his brother.

Mitch took the hawk's feather out of his hat, and readied it at the front door.

"It won't stop the Black Witch," he said in a frightened voice. "Not this time. She'll be ready for it."

Titch darted over to the window and watched the black figure race across the field towards the cottage. Something about it puzzled him.

Mitch stood in the middle of the room holding the feather in his outstretched hand and, although he was trembling, he was ready to face the witch. Then he felt a nudge in his side.

He was surprised to see Titch, looking at him and smiling. Titch then raised a finger to his lips to warn his brother to be silent, and beckoned him to come forward and join him at the window.

When Mitch peeped out of the window, he saw a familiar figure approaching the front door. It was Wendy, dressed up as a witch and trailing a little broom behind her.

"The fancy dress party," whispered Titch to his brother. "Don't you remember? Wendy said she was

going to a fancy dress party, but she didn't say she was going to dress up as a witch."

There was a knock on the door and immediately there came a frightened gobble from under the table. Mitch opened the front door and gestured to Wendy to come in and be quiet. The little girl smiled and tiptoed into the cottage.

Titch pretended to be frightened and, standing by the table, he said in a loud, shaky voice, "The Black Witch is at the door and she wants to speak to Wiffen, the most intelligent turkey in the world."

A strangled voice came from under the table. "He's not here! Wiffen's gone on holiday to Timbuktu. I'm his cousin Woffle and I'm not intelligent at all."

Perry's gruff voice joined in. "I'm not here either; I've gone on holiday with Wiffen."

Wendy clapped her hands and said, in her normal voice, "What a shame. I've brought some strawberry tarts for my friends, Wiffen and Perry, but if they're not here, I suppose Titch and Mitch will have to eat them all."

There was a loud bang as Wiffen's head hit the tabletop in his hurry to back out from underneath. He recognised Wendy's voice and realised he had been fooled. When he stood up and fluffed all his feathers back into place, he glared at the two pixies. "You might have told me it wasn't the black witch coming out of the wood."

"Well, the kettle was right. A witch dressed in black is looking for two pixies, a turkey and a dog. Aren't you frightened any more?" asked Titch, holding his hand over his mouth to hide his laughter.

Perry backed out and looked a bit embarrassed. Wiffen tried to appear unconcerned. "I was just

looking for something I'd dropped," he said. "I wasn't scared at all."

Everybody in the room laughed out loud, apart from Wiffen who scowled, and Perry, who looked a bit sheepish.

After they had all settled down again, they had tea and strawberry tarts and talked about the singing kettle, until finally Wiffen said, "I don't think I want to know the future after all. I think I'll throw it away."

At that very moment, the kettle suddenly started to whistle and sing.

*"Master is coming to get me,*
*He's going to take me home.*
*Put me back where I belong,*
*No more to be alone!"*

"It's not even boiling!" snapped Wiffen.

There was a knock at the door. Wiffen grabbed the kettle and rushed to open it. Outside stood a wizard dressed in a long, blue cloak covered in coloured stars. He had a white beard and a wrinkly face, with small, shining eyes. "Good afternoon" he started to say in a very pompous voice. "I believe you have..."

"A kettle, which you want back!" Wiffen finished off the sentence. "Here it is, and you are very welcome to it." The kettle was thrust into the wizard's arms and before he shut the door, Wiffen added,

"And please look after it better in future. We can't have scruffy gnomes and stray kettles wandering around the neighbourhood. Good day to you, Wizard!"

As the door slammed, the wizard smiled, and held his kettle close...

# 2

# The Blue Wizard's Spell

IT WAS A VERY RAINY AFTERNOON. TITCH
and Mitch had popped in to say hello to Wiffen, as
they often did, when Misty the fairy fluttered gently
down to the front door.

"Do come in," smiled Wiffen, stepping back and
gesturing with his wing. He had a soft spot for the
lovely fairy and would do anything for her. All she
had to do was ask.

"Thank you, Wiffen. It's so lovely to see you again
and I do need to shelter from the rain."

Soon, Titch and Mitch were telling her about the
singing kettle, which Wiffen had bought from a tinker
gnome yesterday.

"It belonged to the Blue Wizard," explained Mitch, "and Wiffen gave it back to him."

"Good riddance," said Wiffen grumpily. "I don't want to know what's going to happen in the future. It could give a turkey nightmares!" He shivered at the memory of yesterday's events.

At that moment, there was a loud knock on the

door that made everyone jump. Perry opened it and called out in alarm. "It's the Blue Wizard again!" he cried. "And the rain has stopped!" he added in surprise.

"Hello there," said the wizard cheerily. "May I come in?"

Before anyone could reply, the wizard, still in his long, coloured cloak and pointed hat, joined the friends in the living room. The rain had indeed stopped and everyone noticed that the Blue Wizard was not even a little bit wet.

He looked curiously at Wiffen and smiled.

"I called back to thank you properly for returning the kettle to me. After all, you bought it in good faith and, discovering its powers, you may have wanted to keep it."

"Certainly not," sniffed Wiffen. "And I never want to see it again either."

"Why did the tinker gnome have it?" asked Mitch.

The wizard sighed, looked a bit embarrassed and

explained. "One day the kettle started singing about a talking turkey that was the most intelligent turkey in the world. 'Absolute nonsense' I said. 'There is no such thing as a talking turkey. All turkeys are stupid.'"

Wiffen snorted, gobbled and his wattle turned bright red.

"Apart from your good self," the wizard added hastily and looked anxiously at Wiffen. "I'm afraid I was a bit grumpy that day and rashly decided that the kettle had lost its powers, so I threw it out. The next day I changed my mind and wanted the kettle back, so I started to track it down. Now I'm very embarrassed to find that the kettle was right, and I have actually met the intelligent talking turkey."

He turned to Wiffen and continued. "It is a pleasure to meet you Mr Wiffen, and to show my gratitude, I shall grant you three wishes. The moment I leave this cottage the magic starts. I hope you will think through your wishes and choose wisely."

"Thank you so much. Would you like to stay and take tea with us," Wiffen said graciously. The thought of three wishes was wonderful and he couldn't wait to get started.

Titch and Mitch were delighted as well, and they clapped their hands in glee. Mitch asked the Blue Wizard, "Can Wiffen have anything he wants in the whole world?"

"Indeed he can, and being the most intelligent turkey in the whole world, I know he will make three very sensible wishes." The wizard nodded wisely and gave a faint smile to the friends as he spoke. "Thank you, but I won't stay for tea. I'll be going now," he said. "Here is a wand that will give you just three wishes. So long as you are holding it, the wishes will come true. It will shrink every time you make a wish. On the third and last wish it will disappear all together. Good luck!" The Blue Wizard pulled an umbrella out of his sleeve and, stepping outside, he popped it open and strode away, rising gently into the air with each step.

As soon as he had gone, the rain started once again, just as if it had never stopped at all.

Titch, Mitch, Misty, Perry and Wiffen all started talking at once. They were very excited and wanted to know what wishes Wiffen would make.

"Oh, let me see now," said the turkey thoughtfully. "How about a cow to live in the garden and give us milk every day?"

"I'd like a bag of bones every day," said Perry hopefully.

"I would also like bigger and stronger wings so I can fly like Misty," said Wiffen smiling at the fairy. "I don't seem to get time to practise flying these days. My wings are a bit weak but I'm building them up with exercise."

"The only exercise he gets is collecting food," interrupted Perry. "He's got so fat he'll never be able to fly."

Wiffen glared at the dog.

"Perhaps you could make the sun shine whenever you want," suggested Mitch.

"I might wish for tail feathers just like a peacock, and a mirror so I can see how elegant I look," Wiffen was getting quite carried away by the idea of three wishes.

"I have an idea," said Misty.

They all looked at her and stayed quiet to hear what she had to say.

"All the fairies and other creatures live in fear of being caught by the trolls and forced to work in the sugar bread mine. I would like Wiffen to help them."

"How would I do that?" asked Wiffen looking a bit apprehensive.

"We travel to the mine and you make a wish that the roof of the mine should collapse and the entrance is buried forever. Then all the creatures that have been made to dig for sugar bread would be set free."

"Yes," cried Titch and Mitch together. Mitch had been made to work down the mine and he was pleased at the thought that it would be shut down for good.

"Well, I suppose that one wish to help my fellow creatures would be a wish well spent," admitted Wiffen graciously.

"All the creatures for miles around would know that Wiffen, the most intelligent turkey in the world, had saved them from the trolls," said Misty, giving Wiffen a little tickle on his wattle.

The embarrassed turkey fluffed up all his feathers and agreed with her. "That's decided then! One wish to close the sugar bread mine."

"I think we should carry out that wish right now," said Misty. "That will give Wiffen more time to consider what he wants to do with the other two wishes."

"We'll go right away," agreed Wiffen. "I am happy to be known as the turkey who saved everyone from the trolls."

"Shouldn't we better wait until it stops raining?" said Titch.

Wiffen walked to the window and looked out. He picked up the wand in his claw and thoughtfully scratched his chin with it. He was keen to get going and said, "Yes, I wish it would stop raining right now."

"No!" shouted Titch.

"Don't," shouted Mitch.

"You'll waste a wish," cried Misty anxiously.

But it was too late. Wiffen had made his first wish. There was a flash of bright light and the rain stopped falling immediately. He looked in dismay at the wand in his hand as it shrunk in size.

"Ahh," he shrieked. "What have I done?" He glared at the wand and threw it to the floor.

"You have wasted a wish," said Misty and she bent down to pick up the wand. "Perhaps I had better keep this until you are ready to make a proper wish."

"You now have two wishes left," said Mitch.

"Perhaps you are not a very intelligent turkey after all. That was a very silly thing to do," said Titch crossly.

Wiffen looked very crestfallen but couldn't think of anything to say.

"Now it's stopped raining we might as well go to Sugar Bread Wood," said Titch, realising that if they waited any longer, Wiffen was quite likely to change his mind about helping all the other creatures. He reasoned that so long as Misty was with them, Wiffen would do as she wanted.

"Now is a very good time," added Mitch, "because we have to destroy the mine when all the creatures have finished their work for the day. It wouldn't do to leave any of them inside. We can hide in the woods until we see all the creatures safely out, and then he can make the wish."

"If we are hiding, then the trolls won't see us and they will never know who collapsed the mine," added Titch, concerned for their own safety.

It was a long walk so the two pixies travelled on
their magic bicycle, Wiffen wore his magic boots,
Misty flew alongside the pixies and Perry was happy to
run alongside Wiffen. Eventually they arrived at the
edge of the woods and hid the bicycle in some
undergrowth. They then proceeded to walk to the
clearing where the trolls lived.

There was a convenient bush to hide behind and
Mitch climbed a little way up a tree to watch for the
prisoners leaving the mine. A few trolls wandered out
into the clearing as the time came for the sugar bread
to be brought to the surface.

"Get ready," called out Mitch. "Here comes the
one with the whistle. When he blows it, all the sugar
bread is brought out. I've met him before. The

prisoners call him Tomato Face."

All the trolls had short, fat bodies with long arms and stubby legs. The one who blew the whistle at the end of the day had long hair hanging round his face

and a large, red nose, which looked like a squashed tomato.

Suddenly the whistle sounded and a sorry looking straggle of prisoners trudged out of the mine. There were two fairies, three gnomes, a badger, four squirrels and a lot of rabbits. They all dragged a basket full of the sugar bread that the trolls loved to eat and stood together in a line. The red-nosed troll walked along the line counting the unfortunate creatures. Satisfied that all the prisoners were out, he blew his whistle again and the prisoners trudged off to their cage on the far side of the clearing, leaving the sugar bread for the trolls.

"Any minute now," whispered Mitch from his hiding place.

The trolls were emerging from the woods and were arguing and fighting over the sugar bread.

"Now!" said Mitch. "Make the wish before the prisoners are locked away for the night."

Wiffen stood up,

puffed out his chest and pointing at the mine he said, "I wish the mine would collapse!"

But this time, there was no flash of light and no sign of the wish coming true. The mine did not collapse.

"Oh dear," said Misty. "We're too far away. You have to be closer to the mine to make the wish work."

"This is quite far enough from the trolls, if you don't mind," said a very agitated Wiffen.

"Come on now Wiffen, you have to go to the entrance of the mine. You have your magic boots on so you can run away when you've made the wish. Please Wiffen, be quick," pleaded Misty. She took hold of the turkey's wing and tried to pull him out from behind the bush.

"Go on Wiffen!" said Titch and together with his brother they pushed at Wiffen's fluffy bottom.

"Let me help," said Perry and putting his head down he charged at

Wiffen. With a protesting gobble and a flurry of flapping wings, Wiffen shot out into the open.

The trolls stared in surprise as a turkey, pulled by a fairy and pushed by two pixies and a dog rushed headlong towards the mine entrance.

When they got there, Misty gave Wiffen the wand and shouted, "Make the wish NOW!"

With the wand grasped firmly in his claw, the turkey gobbled loudly, pointed it at the mine and shouted, "I WISH THE MINE WOULD COLLAPSE AND FILL WITH RUBBISH!"

There was a great flash of light and to the delight of the friends and the horror of the trolls, the mine collapsed with a great roar
of falling stones
and earth. A
cloud of

dust poured out of the
entrance and for a
moment it filled the
clearing. Everybody
started to choke
and cough.
When the
dust
cleared,
they
saw the
entrance to
the mine was
blocked. Behind them

came a cheer from the prisoners who promptly fled in
every direction.

Before the trolls could recover, Titch shouted out,
"RUN!"

The trolls roared and howled with rage and turned
to chase the turkey and his friends who had destroyed
their mine. Unfortunately, as the friends turned to
run back to the wood, a great number of trolls arrived
back at the clearing and blocked their escape. More
trolls came out from the trees and whichever way they
turned to try to run away, they found yet more trolls
coming at them.

Misty fluttered her wings and flew into the air while the pixies, Perry and Wiffen stood in the centre of a circle of trolls, many of whom where waving sticks and shaking fists in a very ferocious way.

Suddenly Misty dropped down next to Wiffen, handed him the wand and said, "You have to make a wish right away."

Wiffen looked unhappily at the wand in his claw. It had shrunk down to a stub because of the last wish. "Oh no, I've only got one wish left," he whined. The distressed turkey looked up as the trolls charged.

"MAKE A WISH!" yelled Titch in fright.

"GET US OUT OF HERE!" bellowed Mitch.

"SAY SOMETHING," howled Perry.

"WISH NOW!" shrieked Misty.

Holding up the wand, Wiffen gobbled desperately but managed to say, "I WISH WE WERE BACK IN THE COTTAGE!"

There was a flash of light, the wand shrank away to nothing and the five friends disappeared. The trolls simply charged into each other and crashed into a heap. None of them could work out where the turkey and his friends had gone.

Back at the cottage, Wiffen turned up sitting on

the floor with his legs stretched out in front of him and a bemused look of confusion on his face.

Titch and Mitch were still clutching each other and trembling with fright.

Perry had his eyes tightly shut, and was lying down with his front paws covering his head.

Misty stood quietly with her wings folded and looking remarkably composed.

"This morning I had three wishes, and now I've got none," complained Wiffen, rubbing his beak sadly.

Misty walked over to him and put an arm around his shoulder. "Never mind," she said. "You have done a very kind thing. I will send a message to the trolls to say they must dig their own sugar bread in future or Wiffen the Terrible Turkey will come back and destroy the mine all over again."

The turkey still looked sad. "No cow to milk," he said.

"No bag of bones," added Perry.

"No peacock feathers and a mirror to look at them in," mumbled the big bird.

Misty interrupted the sad pair, moaning about what might have been. "Wiffen, it is far better to have helped a lot of creatures than just to have helped yourself. I think you're wonderful for doing such a brave thing."

And she gave the turkey a big kiss on his beak.

"Gosh," he said, cheering up. "That's better than anything I could have wished for."

# 3
# The Special Agent

TITCH AND MITCH WERE PLAYING FOOTBALL
in the meadow outside their house when they heard a
loud whistling noise up in the sky. Looking up, they
saw a large, round object hurtling towards them.
There was no time to run away before it hit the
ground with a great crash halfway between them and a
nearby oak tree. Then, much to their surprise, it rose
straight back up into the air again.

They watched, mouths open in astonishment, as
the giant ball bounced high above the oak tree and
then started to fall down again. Only this time, the
big tree got in the way and the ball crashed through
its leaves before coming to a stop half way up, stuck

firmly between two branches.

"What on earth is that?" exclaimed Titch.

"I have no idea," replied his brother. "Maybe it's a meteorite. It looks a bit like a great rock."

"Or a satellite," suggested Titch. "Let's go and have a closer look." Full of curiosity he ran towards the oak tree.

"Wait," called out Mitch cautiously. "It could be a space ship full of strange alien creatures. Let's just watch for a while."

But it was too late. Titch was already clambering up the tree trunk. His brother watched anxiously as

Titch reached the branch
where the strange ball
rested.

"It looks like a giant
football," he called down
to Mitch and poked his
finger into the sphere. "It's
perfectly round and it's got
leather patches all sown
together."

Titch nearly fell off his perch when
the patch of leather he had
just touched suddenly
turned into an open doorway and a
pixie stood in front of him. He was
the same height as Titch and
dressed in a yellow tunic with
black trousers. He had a
bright, smiling face and
long, brown hair, which
reached his shoulders.
Around his neck, he wore
a red and white bow tie.

With his hands resting
on his hips, he looked
around. "Hello," he said,

rather sharply. "I'm looking for two pixies called Titch and Mitch?"

"I'm Titch," said Titch, somewhat puzzled.

"Well," announced the newcomer. "That is excellent! I've found you on my first stop."

"And I'm Mitch," came a cry from the bottom of the tree.

"Unfortunately Bonzo is stuck half way up a tree," said the newcomer with a frown.

"Who's Bonzo?" asked Titch.

"This is Bonzo!" With a flamboyant gesture, the newcomer waved his hand at the giant football.

"And who are you?" asked Titch,

"My name is Jack a' Dandy and I am a special agent."

"How do you know our names?" Mitch called up.

"All in good time," said Jack a'Dandy. "I'm very thirsty. Is there anywhere round here where a hard working special agent can get a cup

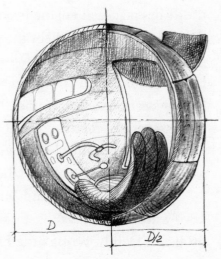

of tea?"

"Of course," said Mitch. "If you would like to come down, we can have some refreshment in our cottage."

Once they were settled inside, Jack a'Dandy leaned back on the sofa and rested a cup of tea on his knee. "I suppose you have some questions," he said.

"We certainly have," replied Mitch. "First of all, what is Bonzo?"

"Bonzo is not a great big leather football as you called it. It is a space bouncer and it was invented by Father Christmas to explore the Earth. Unfortunately, the bouncing up and down made him so sick he couldn't use it, so he gave it to me."

"How does it work?" asked Mitch curiously.

"It has a special engine inside which makes it shoot up into the air, right into the stratosphere, which is very high indeed. When it gets there, it just hovers for as long as I want, while the world down below goes round and round. Then, when I switch the engine into reverse, Bonzo rushes back down to Earth and hey presto, I am in a different part of the world. I can steer Bonzo to land anywhere I want."

"That's wonderful," said Mitch in amazement. "But why did you crash just now?"

Jack a'Dandy went a little bit red. "Erm, slowing

down is the tricky part. Not easy at all in fact. I often get it wrong which is why Bonzo has lots of rubber pads. I always bounce around when I land, that's why it's called a space bouncer. Personally I think it's a design fault, but there you go."

He took a little sip of tea.

"What sort of a special agent are you?" asked Titch.

Jack fingered his red and white bow tie, looked secretive and whispered, "I work for Father Christmas. All his special agents wear red and white ties."

The two pixies looked at each other and leaned forward in their seats. "What do you do for Father Christmas?" asked Mitch.

"As you know, Father Christmas does lots of good work and helps children every year at Christmas time."

"Yes, of course," said Titch. "We went to help him last Christmas."

"Well, he also helps lots of people all the year round, especially his friends, such as pixies, elves, fairies and lots of the little people all over the world. And that's where I come in. As one of his..." Jack a'Dandy cleared his throat, "...Chief special agents, he sends me to help in especially tricky circumstances."

"What sort of things do you do?" asked Mitch.

Jack a'Dandy scratched a small itch at the side of his nose.

"Let me think now... One time, Father Christmas heard that an island in the middle of the ocean had lost all its trees because some men had chopped them all down to build boats. Migrating swallows used the island as a resting point in their long flight from northern Europe down to Africa, but with all the trees gone, there was nowhere for the birds to perch. They couldn't sleep on the floor because the rats would gobble them up, so Father Christmas loaded Bonzo up with seeds to grow trees and taught me a magic spell to make them grow very fast."

"Then what happened?"

"I got to the island just in time. I planted the seeds, recited the spell and the trees grew huge over night. The next day, thousands of swallows arrived and before I left they were sleeping happily in the new branches."

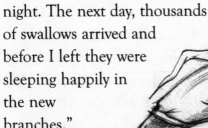

"What else have you done?" asked Mitch.

"Well, last week Father Christmas heard that the black and white beavers in the far north had built a dam and stopped the flow of water down in the Green Pine Valley. This meant that the lake in the valley was drying out and the fish were dying. Father Christmas told me to get there and persuade the beavers to take down the dam."

"We had the same problem here. How did you solve it?"

"Actually it's a bit embarrassing. I went back and told Father Christmas that I helped them to knock it down." Jack blushed and lowered his voice. "I told you it's very difficult to slow Bonzo down when I arrive somewhere."

"And?"

"The truth is that I misjudged the landing very badly indeed and crashed straight into the dam. I destroyed it completely. Then Bonzo and I bounced back into the air and by the time I'd bumped up and down a few times and managed to stop, I peeped out of the window and saw a great crowd of very angry beavers heading towards me. So I didn't actually stop to explain, I just smiled, waved at them, started the engine and flew back up into the sky. But I got the job done."

"How did you know our names and why did you

bounce into our tree?" asked Mitch.

Jack frowned. "I didn't mean to bounce into the tree. Anyway, as you said earlier, you worked for Father Christmas last year and he was very impressed with the help you gave to my friend Red Robin. You know him? Little chap with red hair and red everything else?"

Titch and Mitch nodded eagerly.

"Anyway," carried on the visitor. "He suggested you two might help on my next job. It might be a bit difficult on my own, you see?"

"What do you want us to do?" asked Titch.

"Come with me to the valley of the Weedles."

"Who are the Weedles?"

"I'll explain on the way. Come on, let's go. And bring your football with you, I already have an idea."

Titch and Mitch were excited at the thought of riding in the space bouncer and helping Father Christmas do good works, so they agreed to join Jack a' Dandy on his new mission.

Inside the Space Bouncer, they found plenty of room and they all settled down in the cabin. Jack sat in a special seat for the pilot surrounded by a dashboard with twinkling lights.

"How will you get out of the tree?" asked Titch.

"No problem," said Jack. "We can't go down because we're wedged between the branches, but we can go up and out of the tree the same way I came in, straight into the air. Hang on."

With a great whoosh, the two were squashed back in their seats as Bonzo shot out of the tree and zoomed up into the sky. It wasn't long before they were looking out of the windows and seeing the Earth beneath them revolving slowly round and round.

"We start to come down in about ten minutes so listen carefully and I'll tell you what Father Christmas wants us to do," said Jack.

"In the valley of the Weedles there is a tribe of little people who should be living happily in a lovely land.

Unfortunately, the Weedles are split into two groups. There are the Red Weedles who live on the hill by the valley and there are the Yellow Weedles who live on the hill on the other side of the valley. The Red Weedles wear red pointed hats and the Yellow Weedles wear yellow pointed hats and nobody lives in the valley in between the two hills."

"Why not?" asked Titch.

"Because both groups of Weedles don't like each other and nobody knows the reason why, not even the Weedles. If the Red Weedles go and live in the valley, then the Yellow Weedles roll rocks down the hill and throw stones at them. So the Red Weedles go back up their hill. And if the Yellow Weedles go down into the valley, then the Red Weedles roll rocks and stones down at them. So nobody lives in the lovely green valley."

"What does Father Christmas want us to do?" asked Mitch.

"He wants us to make the Red Weedles and the Yellow Weedles live happily together in the valley."

"How can we do that?"

"I don't know, but that football of yours gives me an idea. Are you ready? It's time to take Bonzo back down. Fasten your safety belts and hang on tight!"

The space bouncer dropped suddenly downwards and the two pixies had to grip their seats fiercely to stop being thrown about. Jack managed to slow Bonzo down just before they hit the ground, but they still landed with a great crash and Bonzo bounced high in the air again. It bounced up and down a lot before finally coming to a stop.

They all peered out of the windows and found they had come to rest in a field in the valley of the Weedles. On either side of the field, there was a steep hill, and as they looked around, they

could see little figures running about on the hillside. On one side, the figures wore yellow hats and on the other side, they wore red hats.

"I see the Weedles," called out Titch. "What do we do now? If we go outside the Weedles will probably roll rocks down on us."

"Not if we wear hats of the right colour," said Jack.

Jack pulled out two pointed hats, one was yellow and the other one was red. "Here we are," he said.

"Titch, you put on the yellow hat and Mitch, you put on the red hat. That way neither side will dare to roll any rocks down on you."

"What will you wear?" asked Mitch.

Jack cleared his throat.

"I won't be going out just yet," he said, adjusting some controls on the dashboard. "The Weedles are very curious and they will have to come down to the valley to investigate. I will make a dramatic entrance shortly. Now off you go and take the football with you. Start to play. It should make the Weedles want to come down to see what's going on."

Reluctantly, the two pixies opened the door and peered out. Titch turned back to Jack a' Dandy.

"If they roll rocks or throw stones, we're coming right back in, so leave the door open."

He then threw the football onto the ground and they both ran down the steps and chased after it. They built two little mounds of stone to represent the goal posts and played at being footballers. When Titch scored a goal, he jumped up in the air and cheered. It was too much for the watching Weedles. Both sides let out a roar and charged down the hillside waving sticks and carrying rocks and stones.

The pixies let out a shriek and ran back to the space bouncer. But, just as they got there, they heard

Jack shout from inside, "Show them how to play properly." Then the door slammed shut in front of them.

They turned round and found all the Weedles standing in two lines and glaring at each other. They wore trousers cut off above the knees revealing short, skinny, hairy legs with knobbly knees. Underneath their hats, they had bushy eyebrows, sharp little noses and pointed chins.

The Weedle nearest to Titch had a yellow hat and, pointing a long bony finger at him, said in a growl, "You have a yellow hat, but you're not a Weedle! You are just one of those ugly pixies from somewhere else. What are you doing here?"

The Weedle nearest to Mitch wore a red hat and beneath his bushy eyebrows, a pair of squinty eyes glowered at him.

"What an ugly creature you are too. You don't have a pointy chin or a knobbly knee. Even yellow Weedles are better looking than you are and they are the ugliest creatures in the valley." Behind him, the red Weedles laughed out loud and the yellow Weedles opposite waved their sticks high in the air and growled in a very menacing fashion.

Titch and Mitch looked at each other for a moment, then Mitch kicked the ball right down the two lines of watching Weedles and raced after it. The Weedles could not resist joining in and immediately all the Weedles charged after the ball as well. The two pixies were bowled over as a great crowd of skinny legs

and knobbly knees raced passed them and kicked the ball as hard as possible. It was chaos. When Titch and Mitch picked themselves up and caught up with the Weedles they were kicking the ball in any direction and charging after it.

Suddenly, a great whistle sounded and everybody stopped in their tracks. Turning round they saw the doors of the space bouncer were open and Jack a'Dandy was standing in the doorway wearing a long red and white cloak. He stood with his hands outstretched and a whistle in his mouth. As if by magic, the ball landed neatly in his hands. He blew the whistle again and shouted out loudly so that everyone could hear him, "I am Jack a'Dandy and I work for Father Christmas. Do you know who Father Christmas is?"

The crowd of astonished Weedles all nodded together. They knew about Father Christmas.

"Good," said Jack. "Because Father Christmas is coming to Weedle valley next Christmas and he will

be bringing presents for all the Weedles who live in
the valley. I said 'in the valley' and not in the hills on
either side. Hands up all those who live in the valley."

All the Weedles put up their hands. "We do!"
roared the red Weedles.

"We do!" shouted the yellow Weedles.

The two opposing forces waved their hitting sticks
at each other and shouted insults.

Jack blew his whistle again and shouted, "We will
have a football match between the red Weedles and
the yellow Weedles. The winners will live in the valley,
and the losers must promise not to roll rocks on them
ever again."

Both sides roared their approval because each side
believed they had the best team.

Jack called out again, "Titch will play in goal for
the yellow team and Mitch will play in goal for the red
team." He then waved the two pixies over to him and
he said in a low voice, "This game must be a draw and
with me as referee and you in goal it will happen. I
have put a magic spell on the ball so you have to
remember some magic spells. The first is this:
'Referoo, Referee, Ball in the air come to me.' Then
the ball will always land in your arms. The second is:
'Referoo, Referee, Ball in the air go past me.' And the
ball will go past you and score a goal."

"That seems easy enough!"
exclaimed Titch and Mitch together.

"Then off you go," roared Jack and he threw the
ball in the air and blew his whistle very loud indeed.

Immediately, all the Weedles chased after it and
for ages they ran themselves ragged trying to score a
goal. Then suddenly a yellow-hatted Weedle broke
free and with twinkling legs raced towards Mitch in
the red goal. He kicked the ball as hard as he could,
but it was going seriously wide of the goal until Mitch
muttered, "Referoo, Referee, Ball in the air go past
me." The ball suddenly swerved on its wild journey
and shot just past Mitch who flung out his arms
desperately as if to save it, but he missed and the
yellow Weedle scored a magnificent goal.

All the yellow Weedles roared with delight and
mobbed the goal scorer who disappeared under a

crowd of yellow-hatted players.

Jack had to blow on
his whistle very hard to
restore order. Then
finally, he started
the game again by
throwing the ball to a

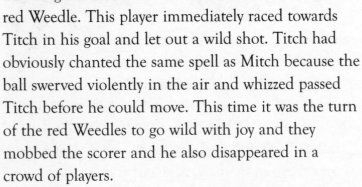

red Weedle. This player immediately raced towards
Titch in his goal and let out a wild shot. Titch had
obviously chanted the same spell as Mitch because the
ball swerved violently in the air and whizzed passed
Titch before he could move. This time it was the turn
of the red Weedles to go wild with joy and they
mobbed the scorer and he also disappeared in a
crowd of players.

Jack started the game again and the red and yellow
Weedles had a wonderful time. They really enjoyed
playing football and scoring goals. Thanks to Titch
and Mitch, after the two teams had played for about
an hour the score was nine all and both sides were in
a state of near exhaustion.

This was the moment Jack had been waiting for.
He blew his whistle and the players all dropped to the
ground for a rest. The special agent walked among
them carrying a bag.

"Father Christmas wants every player to have a

special white hat to mark a special football match." As he passed each player, he took off the yellow or red hat they were wearing and replaced it with a white one from his bag. Eventually, he had all the coloured hats in his bag and all the Weedles were wearing white hats.

A few minutes later Jack blew his whistle again and said, "Come on, its time to start the football match again." He then walked up the steps of Bonzo and waved to Titch and Mitch to join him.

The Weedles tried to line up to start the game again but found they didn't know which side to be

on, because they all wore the same white hats. Players from both sides milled around saying, "Which side are you on and which way is our goal?"

They got very confused and finally turned to Jack for help.

The special agent stood on the steps of the space bouncer and addressed the crowd.

"The football match was a draw, so both sides are winners. That means that all of you can live in the valley in peace and quiet. I am taking your yellow and red hats away with me and Father Christmas will come back at Christmas time with presents for all the Weedles living in the valley and wearing white hats. If you want to play football again, then you can start again tomorrow in the valley. Play every day if you like, but you won't be able to wear yellow or red hats. Here's your football." Then he threw the ball in the air, waved goodbye to the Weedles and joined Titch and Mitch back in the space bouncer.

"You gave them our football!" exclaimed Titch with surprise.

Jack a'Dandy started up the space bouncer before replying.

"I had to. They are better off playing football than throwing stones and hitting each other with sticks, but I have a present for both of you. As well as another football, which I will arrange to have delivered, I have here two red and white bow ties. Father Christmas said I could recruit you both as assistant special agents if we were successful in the mission with the Weedles."

"Hurrah!" cried the two brothers. "Thank Father Christmas for us. We will wear these lovely ties on very special occasions."

# 4
# The Purple Cloak

"WHY IS THERE A GREAT PURPLE FLAG FLYING from the old tree?" asked Wiffen as he arrived one morning at the little cottage where Titch and Mitch lived.

Wiffen, who claimed to be the most intelligent turkey in the world, had had an exhausting journey striding over the narrow strip of sea, which separated their island from the mainland. Titch looked up in surprise as Wiffen slumped on the doorstep and gently rubbed his magic boots.

"What flag?" he replied.

"You can see it from here," said Wiffen, pointing along the path. Titch joined him to stare at the tall,

old tree not far from the cottage. Sure enough, there was a purple flag fixed to the top of the tree and blowing in the wind. Mitch joined his brother and stared at the flag as well.

"I have never seen that before," said Titch. "It certainly wasn't there yesterday."

"I don't believe it is a flag," said Mitch as he shielded his eyes from the sun and studied it. "I don't think it's the right shape for a flag. Come on Titch, let's go and have a closer look."

When the two pixies and Wiffen arrived at the bottom of the tree, they found a number of small animals sitting around and staring up at the flag. Big Jack Rabbit and Willy Water Rat greeted them.

"Hello chaps! I say, look at that magnificent flag."

"But who put it there?" asked Big Jack.

Willy strained his neck to see it better. "It's got silver and gold bits all round it," he said.

"I'll climb up and bring it down," volunteered Titch. "I don't think it's meant to be a flag at all. Perhaps the wind blew it there during the night." He ran to the base of the tree and started to climb up the branches. When he reached the top, he managed to unhook the purple flag from the twig that had caught it. Very gently, it fluttered down to the ground.

By the time Titch returned to the ground, the friends had stretched out the flag on the grass and Wiffen was ready to give his opinion.

"It's a cloak," he announced loftily. "Look at the broad edge down one side and the hood at the other. It's definitely a cloak of some sort."

They all admired the cloak. It was deep purple with a band of gold all around the edges. Diamonds and precious stones sewn into the collar glistened in the morning sun to form a sparkling necklace.

"It's magnificent," breathed Mitch.

"But what sort of cloak is it?" asked Titch, prompting Wiffen further.

"We need to examine this in detail," said Wiffen. "Let us retire to the cottage and see if we can guess who might own such a valuable cloak."

Back in the pixies' cottage, the friends sat in a circle round the purple cloak and examined it.

"Let me see now," said Wiffen at last. "It is a rather small cloak. Perhaps Titch could try it on. It looks the right size for a pixie."

The turkey held out the cloak to Titch and very grandly placed it on his shoulders. It fitted him very well.

"There we are! I suspect it belongs to a pixie," announced Wiffen, sniffing at it and studying the hood minutely. "There is a trace of perfume and I can see long

blonde hairs on the collar," he said
thoughtfully. After another even
closer look he added, "There is a
name tag torn off, but I can just
make out three letters –
LUC....."

Turning to Mitch, he asked,
"Can you feel any pockets in the
cloak?"

There was in fact a large
pocket to one side and Mitch
wiggled his hand in but all he came out with was a
rather large oak leaf.

"Mmm," said Wiffen again. "Does anyone know
which way the wind was blowing last night?"

"The same way that it is right now," replied Big
Jack Rabbit. "But it was more of a gale during the
night."

All the animals nodded in agreement.

"Well, what have we got then?" pondered Wiffen.
"A very valuable cloak, probably owned by a royal
princess, who is a pixie with a name beginning with
LUC. It blew here on the wind in a direct line from
an oak tree and, from the size of the leaf, a very large
tree at that. For a pixie princess to be up an oak tree
would probably mean she is in some sort of trouble.

Now what I propose is this..."

Wiffen never got any further with his proposal, because Budgie the yellow seagull landed outside the house with a bang and a great flapping of feathers. Her head came straight in through the window and she gasped, "The Black Witch is coming! She's riding on her broomstick and flying over the woods right now. Everybody hide."

With that, Budgie flew away as fast as she could. All the animals rushed out of the house and scattered in every direction, leaving Wiffen holding the cloak and looking bewildered.

"What, what, what..." spluttered the confused turkey.

Mitch spoke to him sharply. "Go through the back door and into the garden. Take the cloak, sit on it and pretend to be a turkey."

"But I am a..."

Mitch interrupted him. "If the witch is looking for the cloak and she comes here, she will find it. It obviously doesn't belong to her, so we need to hide it."

"And try and look ordinary," added Titch. "Cluck and gobble a bit."

Bundling up the cloak, Wiffen fled through the back door.

The two brothers were sitting nervously at the table when they heard the Black Witch land in the garden. The sound of her footsteps got nearer and nearer. Mitch started to tremble with fear. Suddenly her head came in through the window and both pixies jumped up with shock. She had a very pale face with a long pointed nose. Black eyes

stared at them and short, straight hair flopped over
her forehead.

"What have we here?" cackled the witch. "Two
wicked little pixies I believe."

Then she roared at them. "You've got my cloak.
Where is it?"

"I don't know anything about your cloak," Titch
quavered bravely back at the witch.

She leered at Mitch and shouted again. "Have you
got it?"

"There's no cloak in this house," he stammered
truthfully.

"Then I'll have a look around if you don't mind."

The Black Witch bustled in through the door and
searched all over the house. Then she went out of the

back door to look in the garden. In the corner of the lawn was a turkey sitting on a patch of straw with its head stuck under its wing and gobbling away. The witch glanced at it but did not suspect that the purple cloak was hidden under the turkey's bottom.

The two brothers stood in the garden and watched her with their fingers crossed behind their backs.

Finally, the Black Witch turned to glare at them and she snarled, "It must have blown out to sea, but if you find it, you have to tell me. Understood?"

"Wh... Why?" stammered Titch.

The Black Witch raised her voice to a hideous shriek and shouted, "It's mine and I want it back. That's all you need to know." And so saying, she grabbed her broomstick, sat on it and flew into the air. After hesitating for a while over their cottage, she flew over the woods and disappeared from sight.

Wiffen's head came from under his wing and he ruffled all his feathers as he stood up. "I didn't know that you were on speaking terms with the wicked Black Witch," he said indignantly.

"We met her once before when she was chasing a little green tree," said Mitch.

"She is terrifying," whispered Titch, his voice still shaking from the encounter. "What are we going to do now?"

"Well," pronounced Wiffen. "Before I was so rudely interrupted, I was about to tell you what to do. You must climb on your magic bicycle and fly into the wind in a straight line until you come to a big oak tree. Somewhere in that tree you should find a clue to the whereabouts of the pixie princess."

"What if the Black Witch sees us," quavered Titch. "She could turn us into toads or something even more horrible."

"Then make sure she doesn't see you," responded Wiffen, showing little sympathy for the pixies. "But of course, if you don't want to rescue a pixie princess, that's entirely up to you."

The two brothers looked at each other.

"I suppose we have to go," said Mitch reluctantly.

"If I remember rightly," said his brother thoughtfully, "when we lived in pixie valley there was a little girl princess called Lucinda. It could be that the letters left on the cloak were part of her name. She was a lovely pixie. We really must go and help her, witch or no witch."

So the two pixies set off on their magic bicycle, with Mitch on the back seat carrying the purple cloak. In a short time, they had crossed the sea and were riding over the mainland and into the wind. After about one hour of flying, they came to a wood of oak trees.

"This must be it," shouted Titch to his brother.

"And that is the biggest oak tree in the whole wood," Mitch pointed to a huge, old tree that appeared in front of them. It rose out of the wood and towered majestically above all the other trees. Its trunk was massive and great long branches spread out in every direction.

"We must land and hide the bicycle," said Titch. "You keep a watch out for the witch and shout out if you see her. She knows us and what is more she knows where we live."

"She must not see us under any

circumstances," agreed his brother anxiously.

Hiding the bicycle under a bush close to the tree, they tiptoed towards the great round trunk and slowly climbed from branch to branch. Pausing every few seconds, they would look all around in case the witch was about. As they climbed, they examined each branch closely for any sign of a clue.

It was Titch whose sharp little eyes saw a small piece of cloth fluttering on a twig near to the trunk and very close to the top of the tree. "Look there," he said with excitement. "Is that part of the name tag?"

Mitch reached out and studied the tiny slip of cloth. "Yes it is," he exclaimed with delight. "There are letters on it which say INDA." He reached for the purple cloak he had wrapped around his waist and joined the two pieces together. "That's it! The name tag reads

- LUCINDA."

The two pixies started climbing down the tree when they noticed a door in the side of the trunk. It was a small wooden door and it  was slightly open. Titch opened it wider and peeped inside. The tree was hollow. There was a small platform with a spiral staircase leading down.

"Perhaps those steps will take us to the bottom of the tree without having to climb all the way down. Maybe we'll find Lucinda," Titch said hopefully.

"Look at that," whispered Mitch, his voice full of fear.

Just inside the doorway was a broomstick resting on a stand. Next to it, an empty stand stood waiting for another broomstick.

When he saw them, Titch recoiled in horror.

"We must be in the witch's lair! Let's get out of here."

The two pixies clambered over each other in their hurry to escape, but Mitch suddenly froze.

"We're too late," he gasped in horror. "The witch is coming! I can see her flying in on her broomstick. Quick, run down the stairs, we must find somewhere to hide."

But there was nowhere to hide on the way down. At the bottom of the tree there were two doors. Titch opened the first one and looked hastily inside. There was a large bed with a table, chair and a small window. "It's the witch's bedroom," he gasped. "We can't hide here."

Mitch opened the other door. It led into a garden. Without hesitation, the two pixies rushed out of the big oak tree and looked all around them.

They were in a beautiful garden, which was surrounded by a very tall wall. All round were flower beds with different types of plants, all close together, some spreading across the ground and others reaching high to spread green leaves and splashes of vivid colours up the walls. In the middle of the lawn was a pond covered in lilies, and next to it was a cage, made of heavy, black iron bars. Peeping through the bars was a beautiful girl pixie wearing a torn yellow dress. She looked very unhappy, but when she saw the two brothers, she smiled and waved for them to come near to her.

Titch and Mitch raced over to the cage and the girl pixie said, "Hello. My name is Lucinda. Have you come to save me?"

There was no time for introductions. "The witch is right behind us," Titch blurted out. "We must find somewhere to hide quickly."

For a few moments, they darted this way and that, desperately looking for a place to hide from the witch.

"Into the pond," said Lucinda suddenly. "It's the best place. The witch hates water!"

The two brothers looked back at the big oak tree. They heard a door slam inside the trunk.

Lucinda called to them, this time there was panic in her voice. "She's in her bedroom, jump into

the pond or she'll see you from the window."

Titch leapt into the pond. Mitch tossed the purple cloak through the bars of the cage and followed his brother. The water came up to their waists and they ducked down so that only the tops of their heads and eyes were above the water. The pond was cold and smelly. As they peered back at the big tree they saw the little window open and the head and shoulders of the witch leaned out. The black staring eyes moved slowly around the garden but saw nothing out of order.

Lucinda had quickly folded up the cloak and was sitting in a chair with it underneath her. There was total silence in the garden and eventually the witch withdrew her head and closed the window.

Lucinda whispered to the pixies, "Stay quiet for a while. She usually has a sleep about now."

Titch and Mitch were covered in mud and they found it hard to move without slipping, so they tried to stay as still and as quiet as possible. Unfortunately,

a number of toads lived by the pond and became attracted to Titch's head. A very large, warty toad swam slowly over to Titch and clambered onto his head by sticking one foot into his mouth, another onto his nose and by grasping hold of his hair. Once he had made himself comfortable, he croaked loudly to all his friends.

Titch gurgled and raised a hand to sweep the cheeky toad back into the water but Lucinda hissed at him. "Keep still, and keep quiet. It's only a toad."

However, as she spoke, three other toads decided to join their friend. Toads' feet poked into Titch's

eyes, his ears, his mouth and his nose.

"Gerroff," he spluttered. "You smell horrible."

But the toads ignored him and soon his head was covered with a small crowd all croaking loudly.

After what seemed like ages, Lucinda whispered to the pixies, "The witch should be resting now." Looking directly at Mitch, she added, "Go and peep through the window and see if she's asleep."

Reluctantly, Mitch crawled out of the pond and, dripping wet, tiptoed across the lawn and slowly looked in at the window. He then returned to the pond and said, "You can come out now. The witch is asleep."

Spluttering and coughing, Titch shook off the toads, removed a tadpole from behind his ear and crawled out of the pond. Standing outside the cage, they talked quietly to Lucinda and told her about the purple cloak they had found and how they had come to rescue her.

"You are very brave pixies. I threw the cloak away when the witch brought me here. It's very valuable and I hoped that someone would find it and help me." She lowered her voice and added, "We have no time to lose, now you must be even braver. The key to the cage hangs on a hook in the witch's bedroom. One of you has to go and get it."

"What?" exclaimed Titch. "Into the witch's bedroom, while she's asleep?" He turned to his brother. "You're quieter than I am, you should go."

"You're older that I am, so you should go," retorted his brother.

"But I'm afraid of the witch and she might hear my knees knocking."

"I'm afraid of the witch as well and she might hear my teeth chattering."

"I'll choose," said Lucinda.

She closed her eyes and started spinning round and round in a circle. Finally, she stopped still and, holding out her hand, she pointed her finger in front of her. When she opened her eyes, it was pointing directly at Titch.

"Oh dear," said Titch forlornly. "When should I go?"

"Right now," replied Lucinda. "The key hangs on the wall by the side of her bed. You must be very, very quiet."

"Don't let her see you," added Mitch,
unnecessarily.

This time it was Titch who tiptoed across the lawn.
Quietly he opened the door in the giant tree trunk
and slipped inside. The door to the witch's room was
ajar so Titch eased it open just enough to squeeze
through the gap. With his heart pounding and
holding his breath, he crossed to the bed. The Black
Witch was lying on her back with her eyes tightly
closed and her large beaky nose pointing to the
ceiling.

Just as Titch stretched out his quivering hand and
lifted the key from its hook, the witch let out an
almighty snore. The sudden noise startled the
frightened pixie and he dropped the key. It fell with a
clatter onto the floor. Titch stood rigid with fear,
staring at the witch in case she woke up, but the eyes
stayed shut and the body lay still. Slowly, Titch leaned
over to retrieve the key, grasping it firmly in his hand.
Then he backed carefully out of the room and closed
the door as much as he dared.

When he made it back to the cage in the garden,
both Lucinda and Mitch whispered excitedly to him.
"Well done," they both said, and Lucinda added,
"You are a wonderful and brave pixie."

Titch opened the cage with the key. Lucinda

stepped out and, for a while, they talked
quietly and urgently.

"You must come and see us in
the valley of the pixies," said
Lucinda holding their hands and
smiling happily.

"How did the witch catch you?"
asked Titch.

"I just left the valley to
explore, but as soon as I
did, the witch
appeared on her
broomstick and
whisked me away."

"We did the same," said Mitch, "but we were
caught by an ogre."

"Where is the valley of the pixies?" asked Titch.
"We've been lost for ages."

"Just follow the wind when it blows to the south,"
Lucinda told them. "But we must go now before the
witch wakes up."

Mitch had told Lucinda about their magic bicycle
and that gave the pixie princess an idea, which she
explained. "The witch leaves her broomsticks by the
door in the tree. I know the magic word to make
them fly so I shall take one and fly it to the valley of

the pixies. When you come to visit me, we will have such a lot to talk about,"

She kissed the two brothers and then ran to the door in the tree.

Just as the two pixies were about to follow her, the toads in the pond saw the pixie princess leave and they all croaked a goodbye together. It made a terrible noise, and Titch turned to shush at them, but it was no good. The toads just croaked even louder.

Throwing caution to the wind, the brothers raced towards the tree. The little window next to it flew open and the witch's head poked out. "What's all that noise?" she roared.

The toads jumped up and down and croaked louder still.

The witch didn't see the pixies dashing through the door, but she certainly heard their feet running up the stairs back to the top branches. As soon as she saw the empty cage, she realised that Lucinda had escaped and, with a howl of rage, ran up the stairs in pursuit.

"Run," squealed Mitch as he pushed at his brother's back to make him go faster. "The witch is coming."

Out of breath and gasping, they reached the door in the top of the tree and looked out. Flying over the

trees and heading south was
Lucinda on a broomstick, her
purple cloak waving behind
her.

The pixies had to climb
down the tree on the outside to
find their magic bicycle so they
could escape. Mitch called to his
brother to follow him and started leaping
down the branches at high speed.

Titch was about to follow him when he spotted the
witch's spare broomstick leaning by the side of the
door. Realising that the witch could chase after them,
or Lucinda, with that broomstick, he grabbed it and
hurled it as far as he could. It bounced on a few
branches then disappeared on its way to the ground at
the bottom of the tree. Titch then clambered
hurriedly after his brother.

The Black Witch reached the doorway at the top
of the stairs and saw that both her broomsticks were
gone. She let out a long scream of rage and
frustration, which followed the two pixies in their
frantic climb down the tree.

By the time they reached the magic bicycle, they
could still hear the witch raging, but at least she was
not chasing them any longer. They climbed onto their

seats and called out the magic words, "Up, Up and Away!"

As they flew through the bright blue sky, Titch leaned back and cheered. "We did it! We rescued the princess and the witch has no idea it was us."

# 5

# The Egg

IT WAS QUITE BY CHANCE THAT TITCH AND
Mitch found the egg. The two pixies were strolling
along the little beach on the
island to see what the tide had
washed up when they came
across a particularly large
clump of seaweed. When
Titch poked about inside it,
he was surprised to find a
rather large, round object,
tightly wrapped up in the
wet strands.

"Come quickly," he

called to his brother. "Look at this. I've found something."

It took some time to scrape all the seaweed away from the object, but finally they succeeded and washed all the dirt off to expose an egg nearly twice the size of a pixie's head.

Standing back, they examined it and wondered where it might have come from.

"The tide could have washed it up from anywhere in the world," said Mitch.

"It's rather big for a bird's egg," added Titch.

"Oh, I don't know, there are some big birds out at sea. There are puffins, gannets, penguins and seagulls. And albatrosses! They're huge!" Mitch stretched his arms wide.

"I wonder if there is a baby bird inside it," wondered Titch. "It might still be alive; after all, the seaweed has kept it quite snug."

"We had better look after it then. I mean, we can't leave it out here can we?" said, Mitch, bending to pick the egg up.

The two pixies carried the egg back to their cottage and wrapped it in blankets. After a few days, it seemed to swell and, when Titch put his ear to the shell, he was sure he could hear something moving about ever so gently.

It seemed that there was a good chance a baby bird was inside and it would eventually hatch out. So they asked their friend Budgie, the yellow seagull, to come and look at the egg in the hope that she would recognise it as belonging to a bird of some sort.

However, when Budgie examined it she shook her head sadly.

"Seagull's eggs are light brown with small dark brown blotches all over the shell. This is white with black spots. It does not belong to a seagull."

"What about an albatross?" asked Mitch, hopefully.

Budgie shook her head.

"I don't think it belongs to an albatross either," she said.

They called in a friendly blackbird they knew. She looked at it and shook her head too. "It's too big for a blackbird's egg," she said. "Much too big. Sorry I can't help."

They sent word to Nena, the owl in charge of the hospital tree, to ask her to come and give her opinion.

Nena arrived in due course but she was baffled as well. "It does not belong to any sort of owl," she said, scratching her head thoughtfully. "In fact, I don't recognise it as belonging to any bird I know."

Soon all the creatures on the island knew that the pixies had found a strange egg and they all wanted to see it, particularly the birds, who each hoped they might recognise it, or even claim it as one of their own. But none of them did. On seeing it, they all shook their heads sadly and said they had never seen anything like it before.

Everyone was thoroughly stumped.

The egg sat in the corner of the room covered in blankets to keep it warm. Each day they examined it and listened to the gentle rustling inside. One day Mitch took a step away from the egg and called out to his brother, "You know, this egg is getting bigger every day!"

Titch joined him. "You're right! It is a lot bigger than when we found it. I have never heard of an egg that grows."

Mitch became quite alarmed. "Whatever is in that egg is going to hatch out in our living room," he said to his brother. "It could happen any day now. What can we do?"

"I have an idea," replied Titch. "Do you remember the little old hermit we met called Cedric?"

"Yes, of

course. He lived in a cave at the end of a rainbow and he had a wonderful book of knowledge."

"Well that book will have information on eggs. It might tell us what sort of a creature will hatch out of it. Because when it does appear, we need to know how to feed the little thing."

"Little thing! If that egg grows any bigger it will be a monster thing."

"Well let's go to see Cedric and look in his book. I'm sure he will help us if he can."

The two pixies jumped on their magic bicycle and shouted out the magic words, "Up, Up and Away."

Straight away the bicycle rose into the air and they set out to consult the book of knowledge.

There was always a rainbow shimmering in the waterfall that hid the entrance to the hermit's cave, and the path leading to it was always wet with spray. When they arrived at Cedric's home, Titch and Mitch ran along the wet path, darted through the waterfall and crawled along the passage to the hidden cave.

To their delight, Cedric was at home, sitting at a table and writing a letter. He was a tiny old man with skinny arms and legs. His hair was long and brown eyes peered out of a wrinkled face. When the pixies popped out of the little passageway his face wrinkled up even more into a big smile of welcome.

"Titch and Mitch!" he exclaimed. "I haven't seen you in ages. Do come in, sit down and have cup of tea."

After they had rested, they told Cedric about the egg they had found that was getting bigger and bigger. He looked at them with a startled expression on his face.

"I have never heard of an egg that gets bigger." He looked thoughtful and added, "This is very strange. An eggshell is normally quite rigid... This one must be growing along with whatever creature is inside."

"How big will it get?" asked Titch with a worried look on his face.

"As it gets bigger the shell must get thinner until one day it will simply go pop and the creature inside will be free. Probably fully grown, if it's what I think it is."

"What do you think it is?" asked Mitch.

"I'll tell you in a

moment. First we must consult the book of knowledge."

They sat round the table and opened the large book. Cedric found the pages on eggs of all sorts. There was a picture of every single egg in the whole world. But none of them looked like the egg sitting in the pixies' cottage.

Eventually, Cedric pushed the book away and for a while he sat silent, deep in thought. The pixies watched him anxiously.

Finally, he said, "In prehistoric days when dinosaurs roamed the earth, lots of creatures laid eggs. It could well have happened that an egg rolled into a glacier and become frozen. Then it would have to wait until it could warm up before hatching. I believe that a strange creature from prehistoric days laid an egg in a far off land that became frozen. Now, clearly, the egg has

been set free from the ice and floated away into the sea. When it became wrapped up in the seaweed it slowly started to warm up and then," he added triumphantly, "it landed on your island and you warmed it up to the right temperature to make it grow."

Titch and Mitch looked at him in horror. "You mean that a prehistoric monster is going to hatch out in our living room," cried Mitch.

"Indeed I do! One day very soon there will be a pop, a shattering of eggshell and you will see a creature from the past. How exciting! Oh, I wish I could fly, so I could go back with you to see this magic moment."

"Magic moment? We don't want a monster in our cottage!" Mitch was quite distressed at the thought.

"Come on, Mitch," said Titch decisively. "We must get back and carry the egg into the garden before it

hatches out. It could be
a fearsome creature and
chase us out of our
own home. Oh no,
that won't do at all."

The bicycle flew as
fast as it could over
hills, valleys, woods,
houses, and finally
skimmed the waves
of the sea on its
dash back to the
island.

"We'll carry it
into the woods and
watch over it until it
hatches. Then, if it's a
frightening monster, we can run away and hide,"
gasped Titch, all out of breath from the journey.

They ran in to their cottage and then stopped and
stared at the egg on the floor of the living room. "It's
too late," said Mitch. "The egg is far too big already, it
won't fit through the door."

"Oh dear," said Titch going quite pale. "It's going
to hatch out here in our living room and there's
nothing we can do about it."

Cedric had shown them pictures of various dinosaurs and Titch recalled them now. "What if it's a Tyrannosaurus," he said. "That's a huge creature."

"Or that wicked looking one with the rows of sharp teeth? Cedric called it a Velociraptor," added Mitch.

The two brothers had a sleepless night as they worried about what sort of creature was going to emerge from the shell.

In the morning, Wiffen arrived. The intelligent turkey had used his magic boots to cross over to the island and he rushed into the cottage just as the pixies were leaving.

"I heard you had a mysterious egg," he said. "It might be a turkey egg, so I need to see it."

They showed him the egg in the living room and Wiffen gasped in amazement. "It's not a turkey egg! It's a monster's egg," he exclaimed. "I don't want to be around here when that thing hatches out. It's big enough to be a full grown dinosaur."

Titch tentatively approached the egg and put his ear to the shell.

"I can hear something. It's making a strange noise. Quiet please."

"It's sort of singing," added Wiffen. "It sounds like 'Gumshoe, shoo shoo.'"

They all pressed their ears to the egg, when suddenly, there was a loud crack and a large lump of eggshell shot up into the air. It was such a shock that Titch jumped back and fell over. Mitch jumped up so high his head hit the ceiling. Wiffen squawked loudly and plumped down on his feathery bottom.

A head popped out of the egg and stared at them.

Wiffen fled from the cottage with a squawk and a flapping of wings, but the two pixies just stared back. The

117

head looked more like a teddy bear than a monster. It had a small squashed nose, short furry ears and two large brown eyes that blinked at the pixies. The head suddenly smiled at them and ducked back inside its shell.

"It's not a bird," said Titch staring at the space where the head had appeared.

"It's a funny looking dinosaur," said Mitch.

The egg started to shake and rattle as the creature inside tried to get out. First, a piece of eggshell fell off the side of it. Then a great chunk dropped off the top and finally it split down the middle and the baby inside stepped out.

It stood upright on two long, scaly legs with large claws on its feet. Its body was a bit like a squirrel, covered with short, red hair and having two arms with small hands and fingers. Beaming at the pixies, it gurgled, "Gumshoe, Gumshoe, Gumshoe."

"What is it?" asked Titch in amazement.

"Cedric must be right... It's a relic from prehistoric days," speculated Mitch.

"It needs somebody to look after it," said Titch. "I wonder what it eats."

"What shall we call it?" pondered Mitch.

"Let's call it Gumshoe, as it's the only thing it has said so far."

They watched as the new arrival took a few unsteady steps around the room, bending its head slightly to avoid the ceiling. It looked long and hard at Mitch, then said, "Mummeee."

Mitch jumped up in the air with surprise. "I'm not your mummy!" he cried. "I don't know where your mummy is but it's definitely not me."

Turning its attention to Titch, the creature smiled happily and said, "Daddee."

"Oh no, no, no," said Titch, "I'm definitely not your

119

daddy."

The two brothers looked at each other in dismay. "What are we going to do with it?" asked Mitch.

"First of all, we call it Gumshoe and we take it outside," suggested his brother. Turning around he walked out of the cottage saying, "Come along Gumshoe, we'd like to show you the world outside."

Obediently, Gumshoe followed them out of the cottage. In the garden, the creature ran around in circles on long scaly legs until the pixies felt quite dizzy. Then he stopped and gazed curiously at all the creatures from the island who had gathered around the cottage to see what had emerged from the egg. They all stared back, faces aghast.

Gumshoe was unperturbed and, spotting a tree at the bottom of the garden, he rushed over to it and climbed rapidly to

the very top.

Titch shouted at him. "Come down here, right this minute!"

"You'll fall," roared Mitch. "Come down now, you naughty dinosaur."

All the other little animals called out as well. "Come down, come down."

Gumshoe stood upright on the top branch and slowly toppled forwards.

A roar of horror went up from all the spectators, but Gumshoe unfolded a pair of short wings from behind his shoulders and flapping them strongly, flew gently down to the ground.

"He's more like a bird after all," said Titch.

"He could be a dinosaur as well," added Mitch.

"There is nobody like Gumshoe in the whole

world!" they both agreed.

Wiffen emerged from his hiding place and added loftily, "He's got turkey legs just like me."

Gumshoe walked to Titch and Mitch and putting his arms around them, he hugged them and gurgled. "Mummeee. Daddee."

"Oh dear," said Titch. "It looks like we have a new resident on the island."

"Yes," added Mitch with a frown. "What are we going to do with him?"

It was quite obvious that Gumshoe would not fit in the house now he was out of his egg and after a few days of living in the garden, his wings grew bigger and stronger and he took to perching on the roof of Titch

and Mitch's house. It made all the creatures on the
island laugh when they came to visit, but Titch and
Mitch found it impossible to sleep with Gumshoe
scratching and scraping on the roof all night long.

Although their new friend grew bigger very
quickly, the only words he could say were Mummee
and Daddee, and to everyone's great surprise and
consternation, he called all the creatures he met either
Mummee or Daddee and tried to
hug them all.

It was difficult to
decide whether
Gumshoe was a
bird or an animal,
after all he had a
face and hands
like a cuddly
animal but he
also had claws
like a bird
and wings
that could
fly him to
the highest
tree. Titch
and Mitch

decided that it didn't matter, he was just a very
affectionate and prehistoric creature that everyone
loved.

One morning Titch was staring up at a high oak
tree where they could just see Gumshoe's head
peeping out of the top. "He likes that tree," said Titch
straining his neck to look upwards. "Do you think
that if we built him a den up there, he would rather
sleep in it than on our roof?"

"We can ask him," suggested Mitch.

When Gumshoe next appeared in their garden
they asked him if he would like a den in his favourite
tree. He tilted his head to one side, crinkled up his
little teddy bear nose, thought for a moment, then
smiled happily and nodded his head vigorously.

"Good," said Titch. "Let's get to work."

In their store cupboard they had an old hammer
and some rusty old nails which they could use. Then
they called on Budgie and Nena from the hospital
tree and explained about the den they were planning
for Gumshoe. Later that day, the two pixies climbed
to the top of the tree and made a platform for the
den. As soon as they finished a great flock of birds
flew in to help. Each one carried a piece of straw or a
twig or a piece of dry seaweed. Nena supervised the
operation and soon a large and comfortable nest was

built in the tree.

Titch and Mitch and all the helpers stood at the bottom of the tree and watched as Gumshoe flew into his new home. There was a shriek of delight from the top of the tree and then Gumshoe's head popped out and two little arms waved happily to the watching crowd.

That night, Titch and Mitch settled down in bed and listened to the silence.

"It seems rather quiet without Gumshoe on the roof," said Mitch thoughtfully. "Do you think he's happy in his tree?"

"I'm sure he is," mumbled Titch. "Everybody's happy on this island. It's what makes the place so special." Then he turned over to get some sleep.

"You're right about that!" agreed Mitch. "It's a very special place indeed."

And, with a tired yawn, he turned down the lamp.